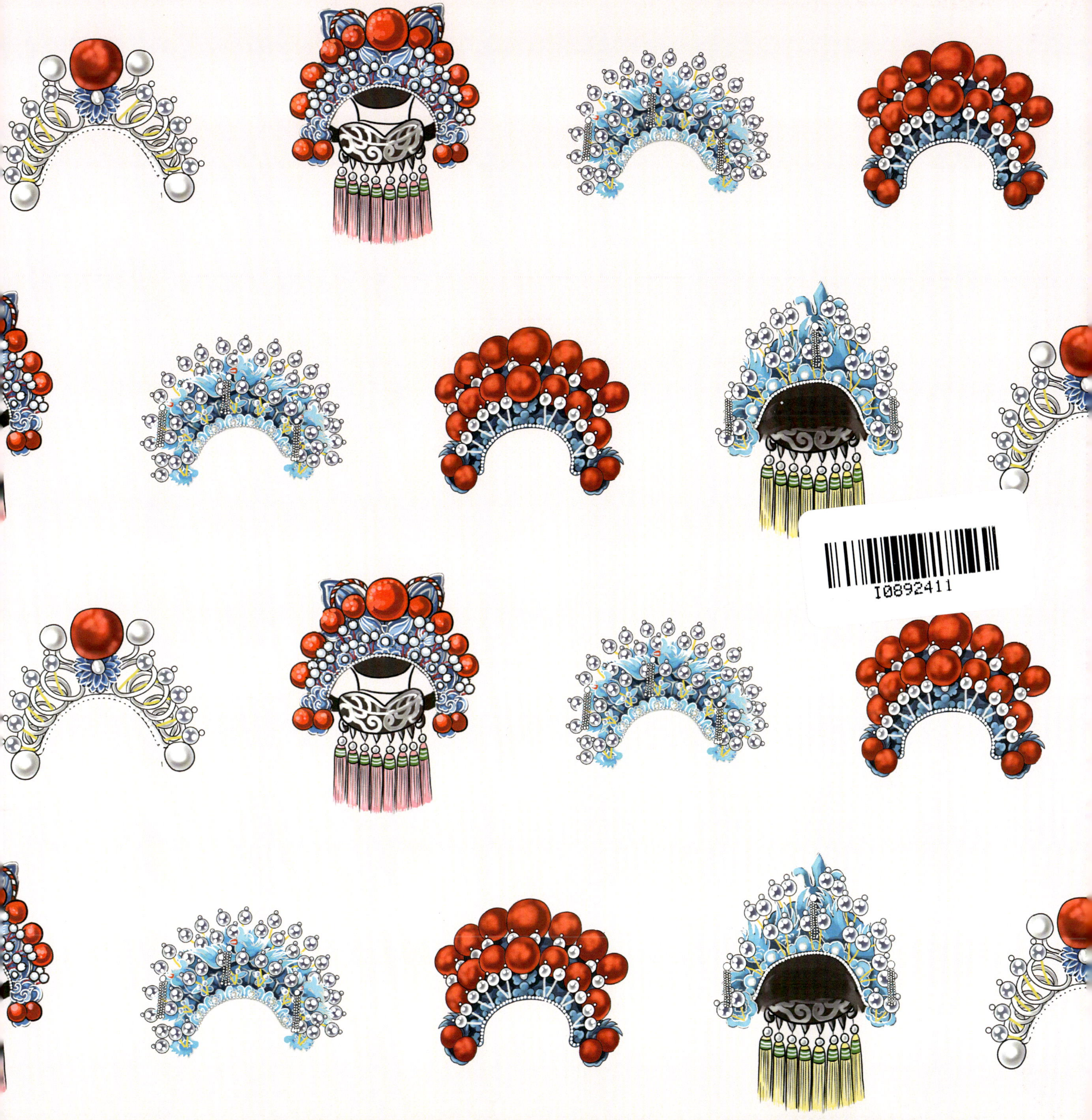

Introduction To Peking Opera

Dan

By Zhou Chuanjia
Illustrated by Pangbudun'er

RC
Books Beyond Boundaries
ROYAL COLLINS

Egg?
Not Egg!

Dan is the name for all female characters in Peking Opera. There are many different types of *Dan* such as *Qingyi*, Floral *Dan*, Old *Dan*, etc. Let's find out more about them.

Princess Tiejing
Hu Sanniang
The White snake
The Nine-Tail Fox
Fairy Maid
Shui Mu
Mu Guiying
Su San

Dowager She
Mrs. Kang
Xue Xiangling
Royal Concubine Yang
Sun Yujiao
Liu Lihua's wife
Yang Paifeng
Liu Yulian
Jiang Qiulian
Wang Baochuan

"Head and Face"

You may have already figured out that "head and face" effectively refers to the jewelry that *Dan* characters wear on their head.

Crystal Jewelry

These are for girls, ladies, and maids from well-off families.

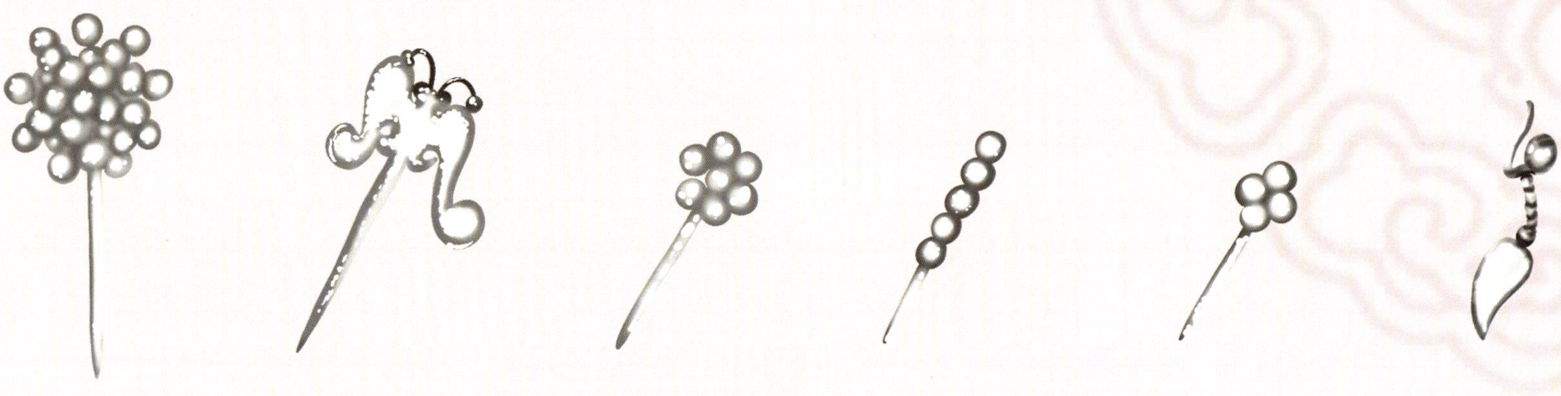

Silver Coated Jewels

Characters from poor families wear this type of jewelry because they cannot afford the top-brass.

Kingfisher Jewels

These are for women from very rich families. In the past, they were made from kingfisher's feathers, which gave them a gorgeous turquoise color. But now we all know it is wrong to take our beautiful friend's feathers for our own use. So, the kingfisher jewelry we see today is made from blue silk.

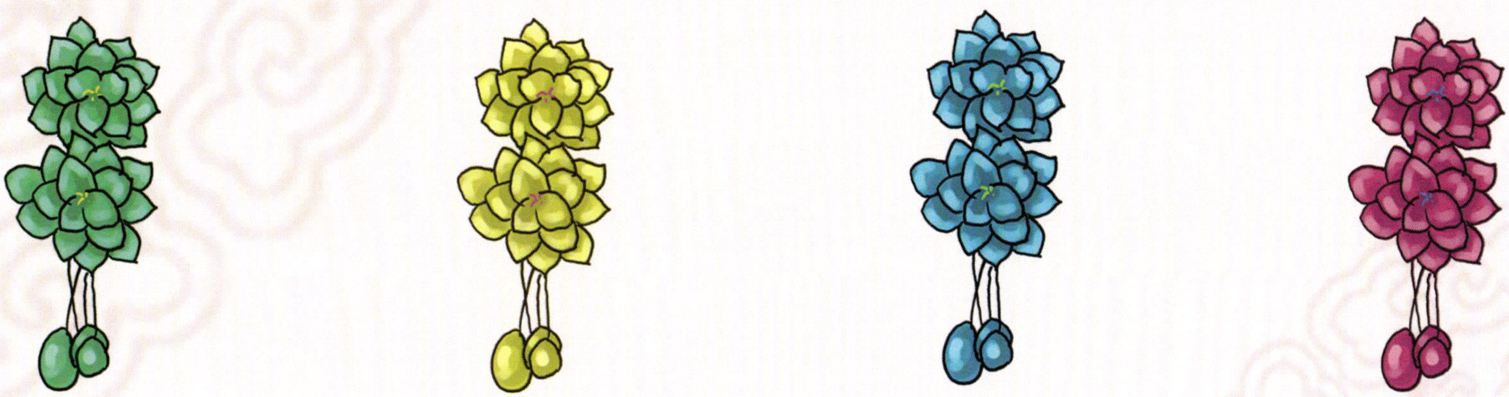

Silk Flowers

There are silk flowers of different colors that *Dan* characters wear in their hair.

Qingyi

This is the most important roles among all *Dan* characters, so we also call it Main *Dan*. The *Qingyi* characters are usually decent, elegant, gentle young ladies.

See, Wang Baochuan is wearing silver coated jewelry. From this, we can deduce she doesn't have much money.

Trimmed Plain *Xuezi* Robe for Women

The *xuezi* robes for women are shorter than those for men. The female robes are usually knee-length, and the actors will wear a longer dress under it. These robes are called *Qingyi xuezi*. *Qing* means black, so *Qingyi* literally means female characters wearing black robes.

Wang Baochuan in the Wujia Hills

Blue Crystal Jewelry

Jiang Qiulian is from a well-off family so she wears blue crystal jewelry. But her stepmother treats her badly, so she also wears a piece of blue silk to cover her head. This means she is living a hard life.

Jiang Qiulian in *The Love Ordeal*

Embroidered *Xuezi* Robe for Women

The color and patterns of *Qingyi* robes are usually simple but elegant.

Su San in *Su San Under Escort*

Fish Shackle

Criminal's Clothes

Su San has to wear these because she is wronged and arrested. The white dress between the top and the trousers needs to be pulled up on the sides. This indicates the character is a criminal.

Xue Xiangling in *Qilin Purse: The Spring and Autumn Pavilion*

Women's Dress

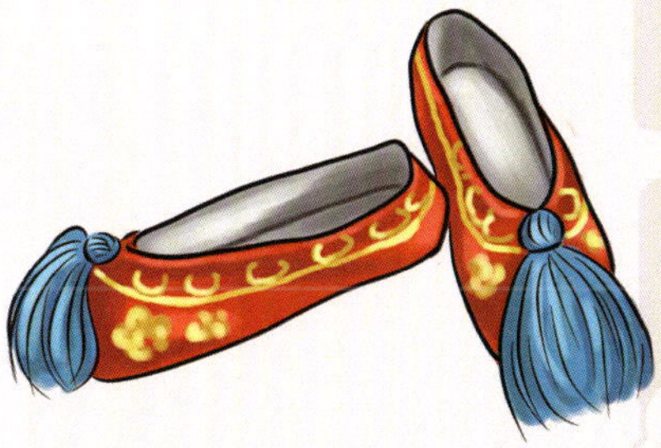

Embroidered Shoes

Shoes for *Dan* characters

Supreme Court

This is one act from *Su San the Courtesan.*

Wang Jinlong, the son of a high official in Nanjing, fell in love with a kind and beautiful courtesan – Su San (also called Yutangchun). When his money was stollen in the brothel, Su San helped him home with her own money, and promised to wait for him all her life. Jinlong studied very hard after he returned home. Soon, in the national imperial exam, he ranked first among all participants and received an official post. However, he didn't know that the bawd at the brothel had secretly sold Su San to the rich businessman Shen Yanlin.

Shen's first wife had been cheating on him and she murdered her husband to be with her lover. Then, she told everyone that Su San was the murderer. Poor Su San was then arrested and escorted to the city of Taiyuan for trail at the supreme court. She was devastated and believed she would soon be sentenced to death. However, she didn't know that the chief justice was no other but her sworn lover Wang Jinlong. He discovered the truth and proved that Su San was innocent. Jinlong and Su San finally reunited, and they lived a happy life together.

Originally, one judge beside Wang Jinlong should wear red and the other should wear blue. But sometimes both characters wear red on stage. This is called "red and prosperous," which indicates the story will have a happy ending.

Floral *Dan*

Different from *Qingyi* characters, the Floral *Dan*s are cute and spirited young girls. Their costumes usually consist of trousers, short tops, waistcoats, and lucky gridles.

Sun Yujiao in *Picking up the Jade Bracelet*

Liu Yulian in *Matchmaker Closet*

Waistcoat

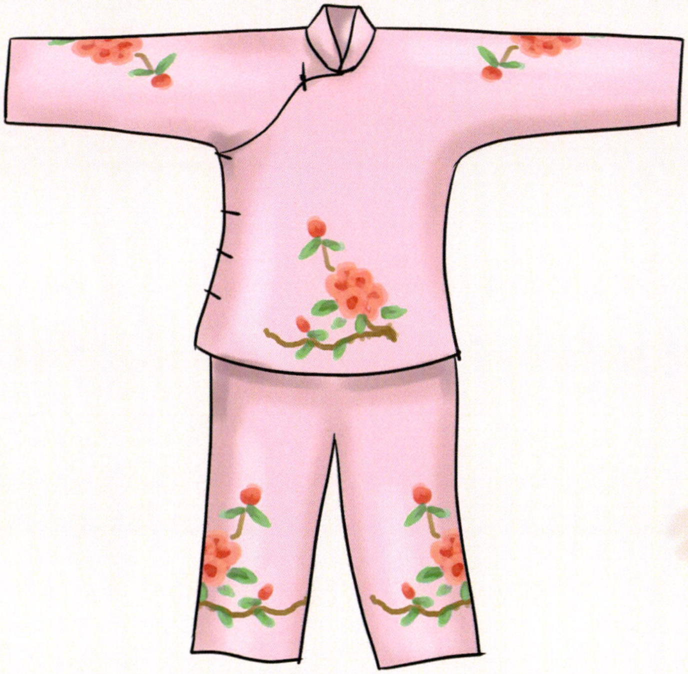

Short Top and Trousers

Lucky Gridle

Picking up the Jade Bracelet

One day, a girl called Sun Yujiao was sitting in front of her house doing embroidery. A scholar named Fu Peng who was passing by saw her and was attracted by her beauty and lively character. So, he pretended that he wanted to buy some chicken and came up to talk with her. Sun Yujiao was also attracted by this polite, handsome young man: it was love at first sight. Before he left, Fu Peng deliberately dropped a jade bracelet as a token before Yujiao's door. When Yujiao went over to pick it up, her neighbor matchmaker Liu happened to come by and saw what she was doing. Matchmaker Liu was enthusiastic and faithful in doing her job, thus she immediately arranged a marriage for the two young lovers.

Huashan

Huashan means decorated dress. *Huashan* characters will usually perform a lot of dancing on stage.

Phoenix Crown

Only women of very high status like queens, royal concubines, and princesses can wear this crown.

Royal Concubine Yang in *The Drunken Beauty*

Dragon Robe for Women and Shoulder Cape

These are formal gowns for women of royal families.

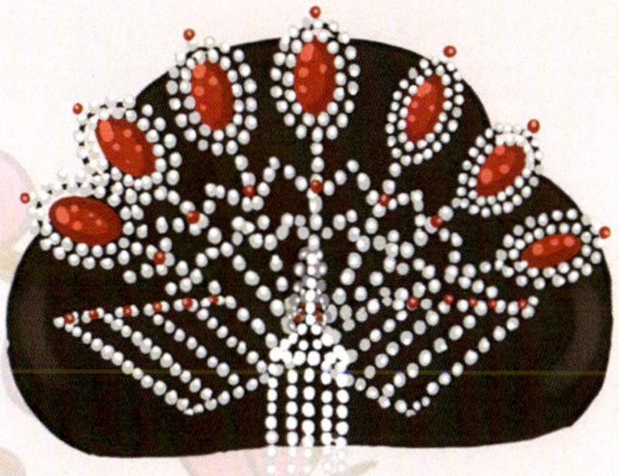

Historical Wig

Historical Robe

Colorful Silk Ribbons

Fairy Maid in *The Fairy Maid Scatters Flowers*

The white snake demon in *The Legend of the White Snake*

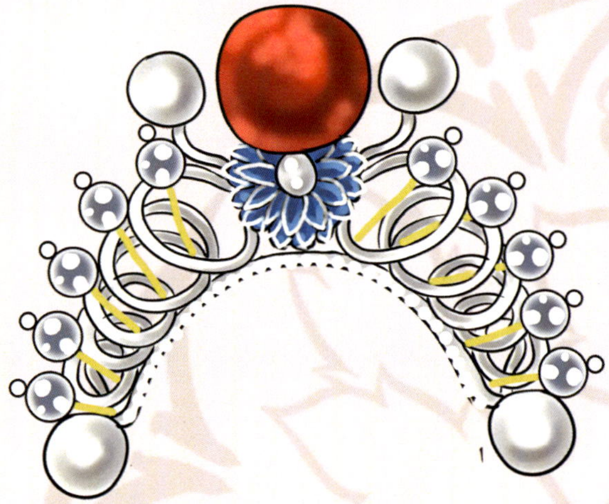

Frontal Decoration (for the White Snake only)

Colorful Silk Bouquet

There are three silk bouquets. The one in the middle is bigger, while the two on the sides are smaller. This is a decoration for elves and demons.

There is one type of *Huashan* character called the *Qi* Costume *Dan*. These characters are women who come from non-Sinitic cultures.

Princess Tiejing in *General Yang Visits his Mother*

***Qi* Costume**

***Qi* Shoes (also called shoes with flowerpot bottoms)**

The Drunken Beauty

One day, back in the Tang dynasty, Emperor Xuanzong and his favorite Royal Concubine Yang agreed to have a romantic meeting at the Flower Pavilion. Concubine Yang put on her finest dress and went excitedly. She waited and waited, but the emperor never came. He broke his promise and went to visit his Royal Concubine Mei instead. Concubine Yang was both angry and sad. Looking at the beautiful scenery under a bright moon, she sang her sorrow and wondered in grief. Soon, she forgot about herself and got drunk. . .

Martial *Dan*, Calvary *Dan*

There are two types of female martial art characters: one we call Martial *Dan*. These characters are great fighters who wear short costumes and usually don't ride horses. The other type is called the Calvary *Dan*. These characters are warriors who wear *kao* armor and fight in wars on horseback.

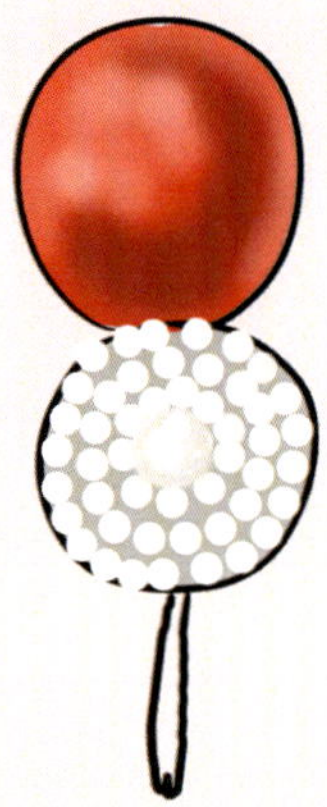

Frontal Decoration

This is usually worn by Martial *Dan* characters.

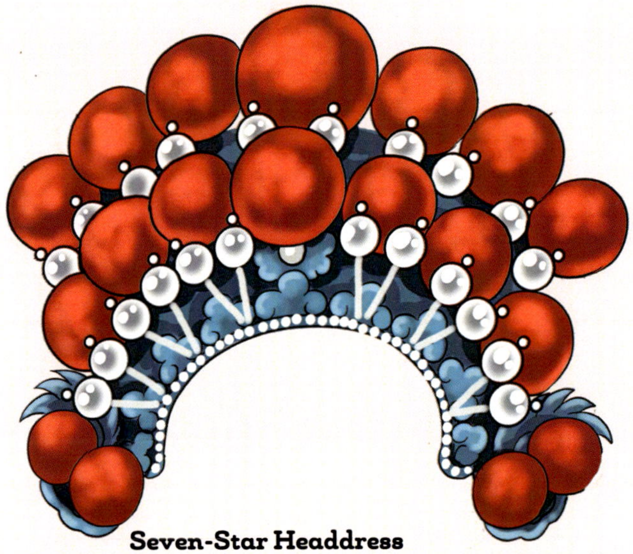

Seven-Star Headdress

This is usually worn by Calvary *Dan* characters.

Pheasant's feathers

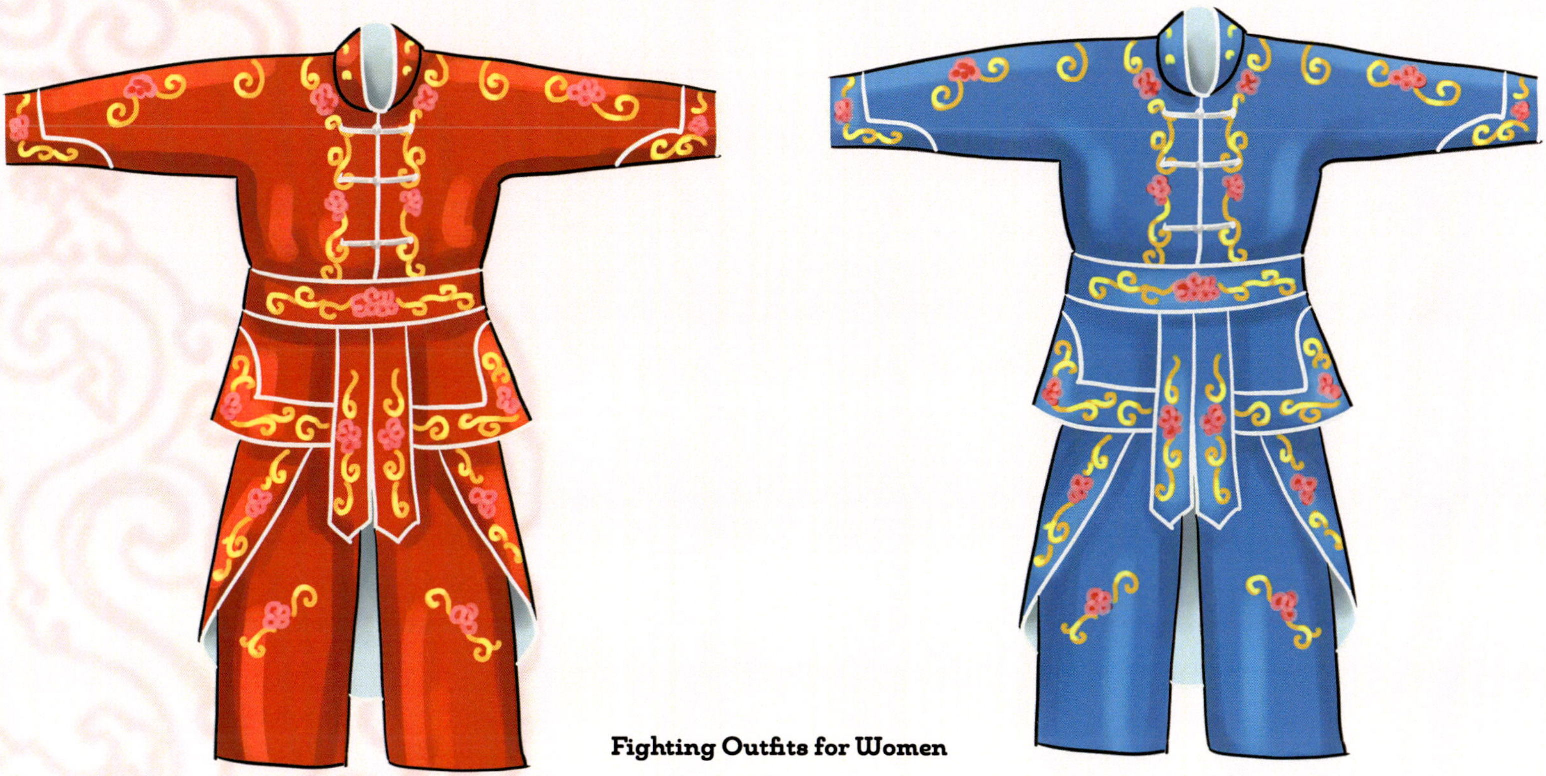

Fighting Outfits for Women

Thin Boots for Women

Martial *Dan*

Martial *Dan*s are female characters who know martial arts.

Yang Paifeng in *Beating General Jiao*

Liu Lihua's wifu

Shuimu the Evil Dragon in *Sizhou City*

The Nine-Tail Fox in *Mount Qingshi*

Calvary *Dan*

The Calvary *Dan* characters are female military officers who wear armor and fight in wars.

Mu Guiying in *Muke Stockaded Village*

***Kao* Armor for Women**

***Kao* Armor Flags**

Reformed *Kao* Armor for Women

This type of armor is a simplified version of traditional armor.

Butterfly Helmet

Hu Sanniang in *Heroine of the Liangshan Marsh*

Muke Stockaded Village

The Northern Song Dynasty (10th–12th century) was at war with the Liao Kingdom. With the Song army under attack, General Yang Yanzhao – the sixth son of the heroic Yang family – sent for help from his fifth brother. They were in desperate need of the spiritual Dragon Taming Tree to expel the demonic forces in enemy troops. The magic tree could only be found in the Muke Stockaded Village. Officer Meng Liang and Officer Jiao Zan both went and requested it, but Mu Guiying, the village leader's daughter, kicked them out.

Defeated and embarrassed, they came back and sought help from the Song military camp. This time, General Yang Yanzhao's son Zongbao set off for Muke Village. However, Zongbao was no match for the skillful warrior, Guiying, who defeated him and took him captive.

But Guiying was secretly attracted to Zongbao during the fight. Instead of killing him, she proposed to him, and the two got married in the village. Officer Meng and Officer Jiao, who were waiting down the mountain, had no idea what was going on and feared Zongbao might be in trouble. Therefore, they set fire to the mountain and tried to make Guiying free their young leader. But Guiying had a magic fan, and she used it to fan the flames back their way. The two officers' hair and beards were badly burned; they had no choice but to return to the Song camp.

Old *Dan*

These are old female characters in plays.

Poor Elders' Clothes

This outfit is for common people.

Mrs. Kang in *The Golden Turtle Took the Bait*

Dowager She in *Women Generals of the Yang Family*

Old *Dan*'s Marshal Helmet

Old *Dan*'s Dragon Robe

Old *Dan* characters of high status will wear it.

Golden Turtle Took the Bait

Old Mrs. Kang had two sons, Zhang Xuan and Zhang Yi. Zhang Xuan was a scholar and he later was appointed the local magistrate of his county. When Xuan's wife heard about this news, she kept it a secret and went to join her husband in the county alone, leaving Xuan's mother and brother behind.

The younger son Yi went fishing at the Mengjin River daily. One day, surprisingly, a golden turtle took the bait. The mother and son were very happy because they never had to suffer from hunger anymore. Then, Mrs. Kang heard the news about her older son's promotion, so she asked Yi to look for his brother. But Yi never came back. Mrs. Kang later learned that it was Xuan's wife who killed Yi because she wanted the golden turtle all to herself.

Mrs. Kang went to Lord Bao, the virtuous judge, and told him what her daughter-in-law had done. In the end, Lord Bao sentenced Xuan's wife to death, redressing Mrs. Kang's painful loss of her filial son Yi.

"Mom, look! Even the droppings of this turtle are silver and gold!"

Let's learn more about Peking Opera (2)

Zhou Chuanjia – professor at Beijing Union University and researcher at the Central Research Institute of Culture and History.

The *Dan* category

Dan refers to female characters in Peking Opera. This role is further divided into sub-categories of *Qingyi* (black robe); Floral *Dan*, Huashan (colorful shirt); Calvary *Dan*; Martial *Dan*, and Old *Dan*. There is also the Colorful *Dan* which is grouped under the *Chou* category.

The term *Qingyi* means "black robe," as this is what *Qingyi* characters usually wear. *Qingyi* is also referred to as Main *Dan* – the characters are mostly positive, decent, and elegant ladies, who are virtuous wives, loving mothers, and chaste lovers. The *Dan* actress performance focuses mainly on singing and falsetto dialogues. Examples for this role are: Wang Chun'e in *The Virtuous Mother Teaches Her Son a Lesson*, Wang Baochuan in *Wujia Hills*, Luofu in *Snobbish Husband*, Zhao Jintang in *Shepherd Wife*, Liu Yingchun in *The Bad Archer Murders His Son by Accident*, Yang Suzhen in *Four Imperial Scholars*, Xueyan in *Martyr and Revenge*, Song Qiaojiao in *The Village Girl Saves Her Lover*.

Women of high status like empresses, princesses, wives, and daughters from wealthy families are also included in this category. For example, Concubine Li in *Requesting a Second Audience*, Empress He in *Empress He Interrogates The Usurper*, Ms. Zhao in *The Sword of Virtue*, Lady Bai the White Snake in *The Orphan Son Mourns His Mother in Confinement*, and Sun Shangxiang in *Badger Game*.

The Floral *Dan* wear short costumes and focus more on dialogues and *dan*ces than on singing in their performances. The characters in this sub-category are usually spirited, lively little girls. For example, there are loyal and cunning young maids, like Chunlan in *Kidnapping the Wrong Bride*, Meiying in *Water Seller*, Chuncao in *Cunning Maid*, Ping'er in *Unsuccessful Courtship Under the Cherry Tree*, Hongniang in *Romance of the Western Chamber*, Chunxiang in *Mischief in the Classroom*, and Yinger in *Loyal Friend and Unfaithful Wife*.

There are also smart and pretty teenage girls like Sun Yujiao in *Picking up the Jade Bracelet* and Jin Yunu in *Hitting the Ungrateful*

Husband. In addition to young girls, the Floral *Dan* can also interpret older women who are savvy, articulate, and carefree. (saucy *Dan*). These characters include: Yan Xijiao in *Tragedy in the Chamber Upstairs*, Pan jinlian in *Adulterous Wife*, Pan Qiaoyun in *Loyal Friend and Unfaithful Wife*, Ma Jinding in *Enemy Becomes Family*, and Mrs. Zou in *Battle of Wancheng.*

One important type of performance for Floral *Dan* actresses is the "Joking plays" they do with *Chou* actors. They usually play jocular, sharp, and frivolous female characters we see in everyday life (joking *Dan*) – like the female leads in *Splitting the Family, Comedy in the Bridal Chamber, Two Henpecked Husbands, The Fake Wooer Becomes the Groom, The Robber Got Robbed, A Maid Marries in the Name of Her Ladyship, Wife Loses the Bet to the Husband, The Idler Miscalculates, Episode on the Journey to Exile, Genuine Friendship*, and *Biting the Hand that Feeds.*

The *Huashan* characters are like an integration of *Qingyi*, Floral *Dan*, and Calvary *Dan* characters. They emphasize all aspects of the performances – singing, dialogue, dancing, and martial arts. Therefore, the *Huashan* can interpret a wide range of characters; some are delicate and quiet, some are playful and cunning, and some are heroic and brave.

This sub-category was invented by Wang Yaoqing in the beginning of the 20th century, and it was later built upon and publicized by Mei Lanfang. Both were outstanding Peking Opera actors of the modern age. Mr. Wang also believed there should be a difference between *Qingyi Huashan* – that emphasizes singing, and Cavalry *Huashan* – that emphasizes dancing and martial arts. Plays with leading *Dan* characters written in the 20th century were mostly tailored for the *Huashan*. These include: *The Drunken Beauty, Saving the Filial Mermaid Girl, Fairy Maid Scatters Flowers, The Hegemon-King Bids His Lady Farewell and The Bandit Girl Becomes a Female General* by Mei Lanfang; *A False Portrait, The Lowly Sage Disciple, Princess Shuangyang the Warrior's Wife, Reunion of Mother and Son, and Nineteen Swordsmen of Qingcheng* by Shang Xiaoyun; *The Tragedy of the Barren Mountain, The Forgotten Lover, Qilin Purse, Sing-Song Girl's Elopement, The Jade Hair Pin's Conspiracy, and, Yingtai Defies Her Marriage* by Cheng Yanqiu; *The Yo Sisters in the Red Chamber The Matchmaker Maid, The Poor Abandoned Wife, The Guilty Silk Ribbon*, and *Warrior Girl* by Xun Huisheng.

Also, there is another group of *Dan* characters we haven't mentioned yet: the *Qi* Costume *Dan*, like Princess Tiejing and Empress Xiao in *General Yang Visits His Mother*, and Wang Xifeng in *The Yo Sisters in the Red Chamber*. They wear a distinctive "two-handful" hairstyle, the *Qi* costume, and flower-pot-bottom shoes. They perform *Jing-Yun* dialogues.

Cavalry *Dan* interpret young female figures who are adept in martial arts. They wear *kao* armor, ride horses, use long weapons, and focus both on singing and martial art performances. Examples are: Mu Guiying in *Muke Stockade Village*, Liang Hongyu in *Battle of Jinshan*, He Yufeng in *Ms. Rescuer*, Hu Sanniang in *Heroine of the Liangshan Marsh*, and Mrs. Dongfang in *Nihong Pass*.

Martial *Dan* characters are also skilled fighters, but their performances emphasize martial arts alone. Unlike the Calvary *Dan*, Martial *Dan* wear short outfits, reformed soft armor, and waist scarfs. They are trained for various techniques such as strikes, handstands, wrestles, somersaults, acrobatics, squat walks, and stilt walking. Some "original adept plays" for Martial *Dan* include: Sun Erniang in *Shizi Hills*, Bao Jinhua in *Yu Qian Saves His Master*, Shuimu the Evil Dragon in *Sizhou City*, Zhang Yue'e in *The Bandit Couple*, Tao Sanchun in *No Discord, No Concord*, and the crocodile demon in *The Feast of Celestial Peaches*.

Old *Dan* characters are normally elderly women with grey or white hair. The actors don't use falsetto either in singing or in dialogues, and their makeup is also light. Some Old *Dan* characters focus on singing, like Mrs. Kang in *The Golden Turtle Took the Bait and The Murdered Son Visits His Mother in Her Dream*, Dou Taizhen in *Empress Dou Yearns for Her Son in War*, Concubine Li in *Lord Bao Hails the Exiled Empress in Court/Empress Li Punishes Her Son,* Dowager She in *Dowager She Resigns Her Post in Court* and *General Yang Visits His Mother*, Lady Xu in *Hostage*, Liu Qingti in *Tortures in Hell* and *Ghost's Remorse*, Mrs. Wu in *Auspicious Wedding*, Lady Wang in *Xue Pinggui Ascends the Throne*, and Mrs. Ke in *The Snobbish Husband*.

Others focus on acting, like Mrs. He in *The Adopted Son*, Lady Di in *Lovers in War*, Lady Zhu in *The Shepherd Wife*, and Dowager She in *Yanmen Pass*.

About the Author:

Zhou Chuanjia was born in 1944. He studied at Peking University and Chinese National Academy of Arts, where he received his doctorate in literature. Zhou is a professor at Beijing Union University, a researcher at the Central Research Institute of Culture and History, and an expert who enjoys the special allowance of the State Council. Zhou has been teaching and researching Chinese literature, opera history, and opera critique for a long time. His major publications include *Introduction to Opera Script Writing*, *Performance of Famous Dan Actors*, and *Opera: Chinese Cultural Elements.*

About the Illustrator:

Pangbudun'er is an independent writer and painter of the post-80s generation. His work is engaging with its own unique style. He painted illustrations for *Fun Talks on the Three Kingdoms* by Cai Kangyong and Hou Wenyong; his other publications include *Raising the Curtains: Will you Hear Some Peking Opera?* and several Peking Opera picture books such as *Protecting the Protected* and *Empty Fort Strategy.*

Introduction To Peking Opera:
Dan

By Zhou Chuanjia
Illustrated by Pangbudun'er

First published in 2022 by Royal Collins Publishing Group Inc.
Groupe Publication Royal Collins Inc.
BKM Royalcollins Publishers Private Limited

Headquarters: 550-555 boul. René-Lévesque O Montréal (Québec) H2Z1B1 Canada
India office: 805 Hemkunt House, 8th Floor, Rajendra Place, New Delhi 110 008

ISBN: 978-1-4878-0912-6

To find out more about our publications, please visit www.royalcollins.com.